First printing, 2020.

1 2 3 4 5 6 7 8 9 10

Published in Canada by The Whamdoozer Company
Box 6636, Fort St. John, BC, Canada, V1J 4J1

ISBN 978-1-7772251-2-4

hookersandblowbooks.com

Hookers and Blow

SAVE CHRISTMAS

Written & Illustrated by Munty C. Pepin

The snow was quite deep
and covered the road.
Blow got to work blowing
and could handle the load.

They travelled down Main Street
and straight out of town.
Drove up on Mount Dexter
then all the way down.

Just 'round the bend
Tom Transport soon did appear,
all covered in snow,
right up to his mirrors.

Blow cleared away the snow,
it didn't take long.
Now Hookers could check
what might have gone wrong.

CPSIA information can be obtained
at www.ICGtesting.com
Printed in the USA
BVRC102115171221
624418BV00003B/56

* 9 7 8 1 7 7 7 2 2 5 1 2 4 *